My Hijab
is Puffy

Written by Nakia L

Illustrated by Sumayyah Syed

PEARLS OF JANNAH PRESS EST. 2022

My Hijab is Puffy
Copyright © 2022 by Nakia L. Cook

For more information, contact nakia@nakiacook.com.

First edition April 2022
Pearls of Jannah Press

ISBN 978-1-7774039-4-2 (paperback)

www.pearlsofjannahpress.com

This book is dedicated to my children,
Maryam, Ibrahim, Sumayyah,
Khadijah, and Nusaybah.
May Allah keep you on the right path,
ameen.

My hair is thick and strong;
If you pull it tight, it's very long.

Natural curls, ponytail or braid,
Under my hijab, they're nicely laid.

I'm running late,
And the school bus is near.

My room is in such disarray,
I haven't put my clothes away.

I wade through the laundry, here and there,
I can't find any good clothes to wear.

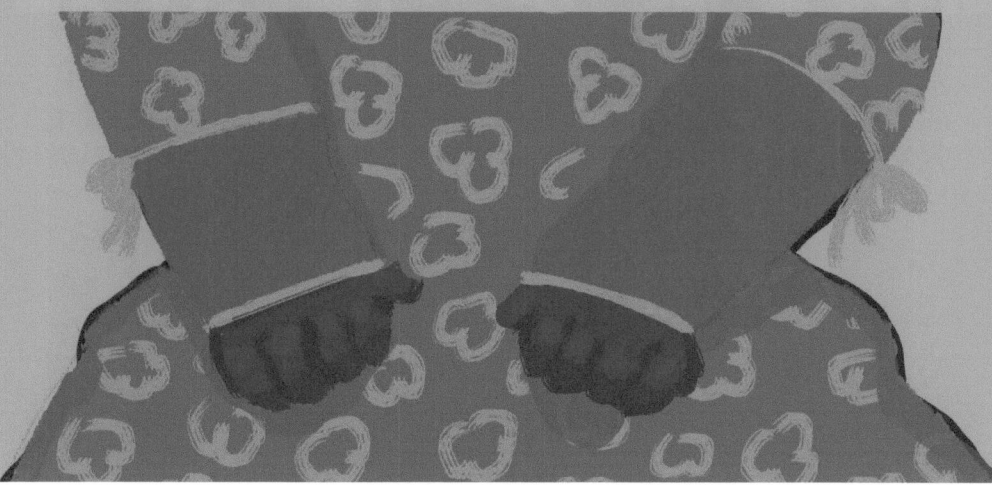

A wrinkled dress is the first thing I grab,
Along with my favorite yellow hijab.

The patterns make an awful clash,
But there's no time, I have to dash.

Underneath, my hair is all in a tangle,
My hijab sticks out from every angle.

My clothes are wrinkled, my hair is fluffy,
But worst of all, my hijab is puffy!

The bus driver smiles with nary a smirk,
As I climb aboard, it's difficult work.

I walk through the aisle to obtain a seat,
I feel embarrassed, and not very neat.

As I take my hands and squish down my curls,
I ignore the laughs and jokes from the girls.

When we get to school, no one is talking,
I walk on by, while they stand there gawking.

I wobble, bobble and walk through the door,
My cheeks burn scarlet, my eyes watch the floor.

I stumble and bumble, then sit on my chair,
And pat down the bulges of dense, curly hair.

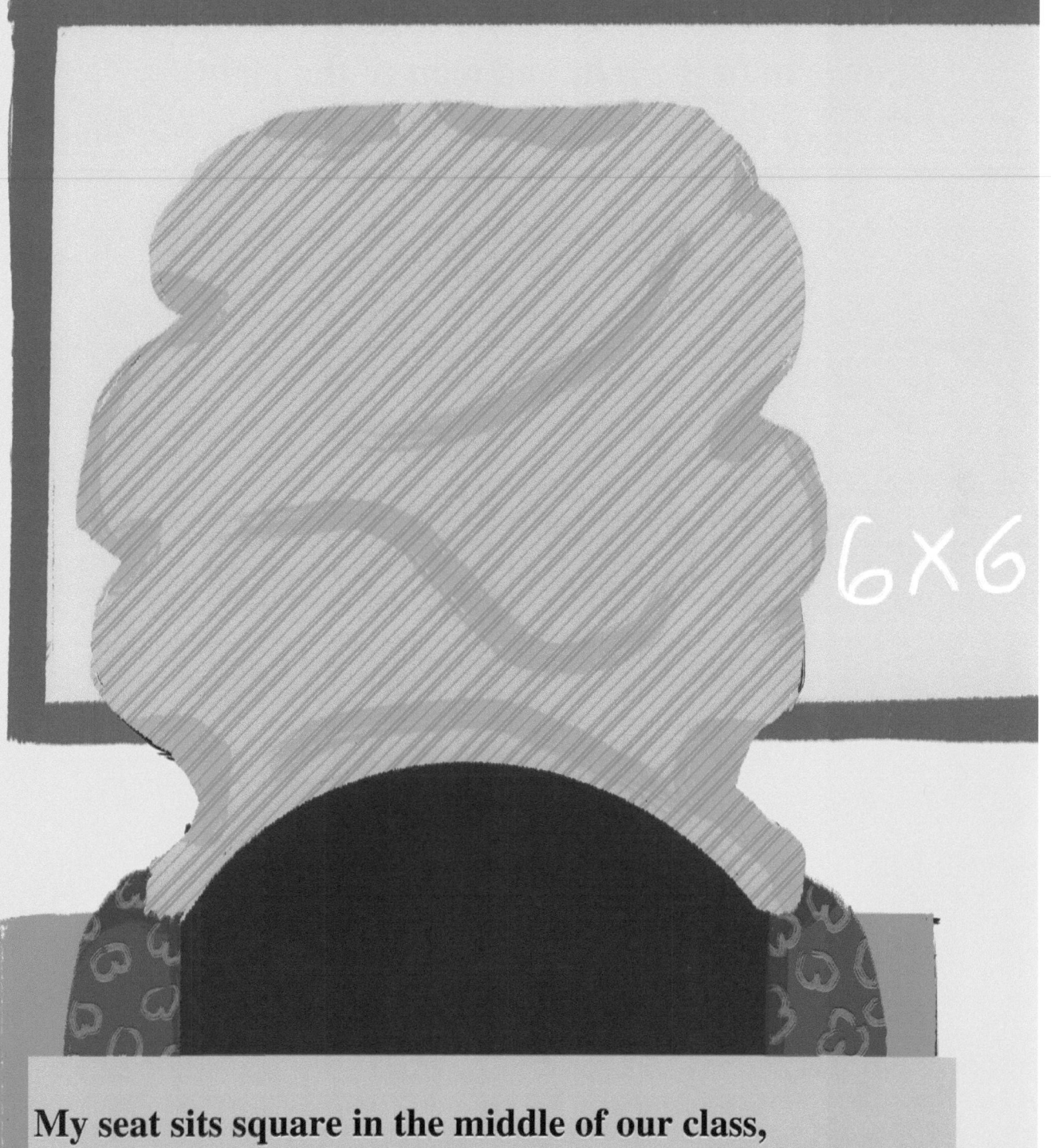

My seat sits square in the middle of our class,
"Please move your head, Noora, it's not made of glass."

They lean to the left, and lean to the right,
"We can't see the board, you're blocking our sight."

While our teacher prepares our daily tasks,
Layla leans over and quietly asks,

"Perhaps you can use my hair elastic?"
"Shukran Layla, that would be fantastic."

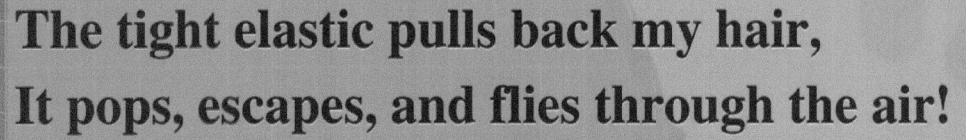

The tight elastic pulls back my hair,
It pops, escapes, and flies through the air!

Yusra leans over and sticks out her hand,
"Since that didn't work, try my rubber band."

Success! We've managed to smooth out the back.
Our teacher looks up, "Are you keeping track?"

Adeelah tosses her headband to me,
But the fabric's too thin, weak and flimsy.

It stretches beyond its limit and pops,
My hair wins again, it puffs out and drops.

"Noora, try my hair bow, I think it's the best,"
Says Marwa, as she tries to help tame my nest.

She hands it to me, I take it and sigh,
"Don't worry, Noora, just give it a try."

"I have one for you, and it's heavy duty,"
Iman says to me, sincerely and truly.

And just like the others turned out to be,
Marwa and Iman are thoughtful to me.

I tie my hair back, and smooth it all down,
My hijab adorns my head like a crown.

My friends are so kind, and showed me they care.
Alhamdulillah, they offered to share.

My clothes may be wrinkled,
My hair is still fluffy,

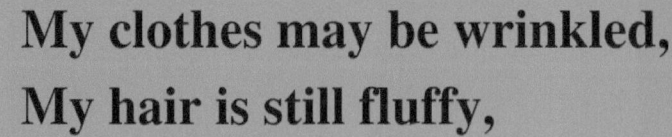

But thanks to great friends,
My hijab is not puffy.

Glossary

Shukran: Thank you

Alhamdulillah: Praise be to God, (Allah).

The End

Acknowledgements

To Maryam Syed: Without you, there would be no illustrations or illustrator. Thank you for being a great sibling!

About the Author

Nakia L. Cook is an American expat living in Canada with her husband and five children. She homeschools and also writes novels for grownups that are too spooky for kids!

About the Illustrator

Sumayyah Syed is a fifteen-year-old illustrator from Canada. When she's not busy drawing, she's doing homework while putting up with her brother and three sisters!

If you liked our story, please leave a review. We appreciate your support.

Milton Keynes UK
Ingram Content Group UK Ltd.
UKHW050317130224
437742UK00002B/71